CAMPFIRE STORIES
FOR AN EVOLVING WORLD

Publisher's Cataloging-in-Publication data

Names: Valen, Genie, author. | Cook, Leslie, illustrator.

Title: Campfire stories for an evolving world / written by Genie Valen ; illustrated by Leslie Cook.

Description: Santa Fe, NM: Little Horse Productions, 2021.

Identifiers: LCCN: 2021917676 | ISBN: 978-1-7373294-0-4 (paperback) | 978-1-7373294-1-1 (ebook)
Subjects: LCSH Storytelling. | Self-actualization (Psychology)--Juvenile fiction. | Conduct of life--Juvenile fiction. | Self-esteem--Juvenile fiction. | Short stories. | BISAC JUVENILE FICTION /General | JUVENILE FICTION / Legends, Myths, Fables / General
Classification: LCC PZ7.1 .V332 Ca 2021 | DDC [Fic]--dc23

First published by Little Horse Productions in 2021
Author: Genie Valen
Illustrator: Leslie Cook
Edited By: Peggy O'Mara
Book Design By: Adam Robinson
for Good Book Developers

For more information or bulk sales, please visit
LITTLEHORSEPRODUCTIONS.COM

Campfire Stories

for an

Evolving World

Genie Valen

Illustrations by Leslie Cook

For our younger generations.

May you lead with compassion
and connection to all creation.

AUTHOR'S NOTE...

In the 1980s, when I lived in Los Angeles, I had the good fortune to be introduced to an amazing woman, MaryAnna Selley. She was an artist, a poet, and a psychic. After years of her acquaintance filled with many amazing visits, phone calls, and profound bits of writing, she gave me a long silver chain necklace with a large key as its pendant. She said, "Here's one of the keys," and then she handed me a scrap of paper with a message—Love is the First Key. I wondered what the other keys were as I placed the necklace and note aside. My first thanks goes to MaryAnna who planted a seed that finally sprouted after thirty five years.

I believe that stories are autobiographical; even when we are not talking about ourselves we are at least talking through our personal filters. These stories are inspired by the most important people and beliefs in my life. I thank you all for your presence and inspiration. Special thanks goes to Patrick Singleton, Leslie Cook, Marian Urban, Peggy O'Mara, Adrienne Reeves, Helen Morales, and especially my parents Jack Cook (In His Brothers' Footsteps), and Bess Cook, (The Rose Colored Glasses).

If every cloud has its silver lining, then every silver lining is a doorway to transformation.

TABLE OF CONTENTS

THE CAMPFIRE

D AD PACED AROUND THE KITCHEN WHILE Mom sat at the table wondering if she had convinced him. He had a decision to make. Should we stay or leave? At least, the question of where was easily answered. With tear stained cheeks, my brother and I waited for Dad's decision. Instinctively, we knew that the family cabin high in the mountains was the safest place to be. Dad finally looked up at our expectant faces and nodded his agreement. Gratefully, Mom stood to embrace our father. They both knew she was usually right, especially when it came to the family's safety. With yelps of excitement, my brother and I raced to our rooms to pack the one bag we each were allowed to take.

Two hours later the pickup truck was packed and ready to go. My brother and I squeezed into the small back seat with our pillows between us. Our family packed for a long stay, and we couldn't wait to leave the city behind. The skies were darkening from the black cloud hovering over most of the land. It was a cloud of negativity, disease, and ill will. We could have hunkered down in our city house, but the mountains offered fresh air and a new perspective. As we traveled high into the mountains, the sky, as well as our moods, lightened. This was the right decision, the first of many to come.

Later that night, after unpacking, Dad made a fire in a clearing in front of the cabin. It was a large fire and provided the comfort we all needed. My brother and I sat on either side of Mom leaning into the safety of her arms. Dad sat a little apart with his head bowed and his hands covering his face. He preferred the inner darkness as he searched for answers to his most important questions. How was he to prepare his son and daughter for such an uncertain world? We couldn't stay here forever. We could wait out the worst of the world's troubles, but at some point we would need to go back and join society, once again. So Dad prayed for guidance, searching the inner darkness for a point of light or a whisper of hope.

"Dad, look!" I exclaimed. Dad's head jerked up, his eyes temporarily blinded by the firelight. We all stared across the campfire at the figure of an older woman sitting as if she were a member of the family. It might have been a frightening moment except for her kind and sympathetic expression.

"Who are you?" Dad stammered.

"I am the Storyteller," she answered, "and I was sent to give you the keys to your prayers."

"Are you real?" I asked.

"I am as real as you want me to be," she replied again. "But the real truth is in the keys. They will help you navigate a new world."

We were all astounded as the Storyteller lifted her arms, summoning a group of figures behind her.

"These are my companions," she explained. "Each night, one will join you around this fire, give you the gift of their story, and leave you with a key. Once all have told their stories, you will possess the keys you need."

We looked at the vague figures behind her. There was a young woman with a sword, a kind looking man holding a lizard, and another woman clutching a beam of light. There was a girl with her dog, and two sisters arm in arm—one with a butterfly and one with a pair of rose colored glasses. A large cat sat majestically next to a pond of water. A man carried a pole across his shoulders and two brothers stood side by side. There was a couple sitting together with a loving cat in their arms, a woman with a crown on her head, and another woman who was old and frail. We also saw a Greek Goddess standing beside a single dandelion and gazing at her reflection in the mirror she was holding. We strained to clearly see the figures just beyond the light.

"Remember," the Storyteller said, "you will be visited by one each night as you sit around this fire." With those words, they all faded into darkness. My brother and I jumped up from our seats to explore and we found the first key lying on the ground. We brought the key to our father, and when he examined it, he found an inscription—"Ask and You Will Receive." That night my brother and I took turns placing the key under our pillows.

The next night, as our family sat around the campfire, the first figure appeared. As long as the young woman with the sword was telling her story, she seemed as real as we were. When she was finished, she faded into darkness. Every night a different figure appeared to tell a story, and each time we found a new key on the ground. As the stories continued, Dad stood a little taller, his brow less furrowed. Mom relaxed her worried embraces and enveloped our family with love. My brother and I grew strong and healthy with glowing cheeks and hearts full of laughter.

So listen closely to these stories with my family. Discover the keys for yourself, and embrace what they have to offer. Stand tall, face the world with love, and let your heart be light with healing laughter.

~ ~ ~ KEY to a New World ~ ~ ~

Ask And You Will Receive

Dragon's Breath

ALLY LEFT THE ACCOUNTING FIRM promptly at five. She had watched the clock for the last half hour, counting the minutes. Now, as she walked to the bus stop, she wondered if she had any energy left for something creative. This was not how she envisioned her life. How did she get stuck in a windowless office when she once had such an adventurous spirit? There had been other opportunities, but she never allowed herself to pursue them. Besides, what did it matter? She had already given up on her dreams. She climbed into bed early that evening; sleep would be a welcome escape. It wasn't long before she drifted off.

The last thing she remembered was falling asleep to ocean waves crashing on the surf, one of the channels on her new sound machine. It was a gift she gave to herself to help with sleepless nights. Now, in a dream, Ally walks through a dense fog with no idea where she is. The thick, moist atmosphere offers a visibility ripe with figments of her imagination. She tires of straining her eyes to make sense of something, anything, solid. As she closes them, she hears a faint, distant sound. She listens through the fog, and realizes that the distant sound is the crashing of waves on the shore. The fog thins as the waves become louder, and suddenly, she is standing on a vast stretch of beach. The sky is many shades of grey with no sun in sight. Mist from crashing waves rises to meet the fog encircling her. She turns to look, curious to see from where she has come.

Ally is reminded of a special name she knows for the fog: Dragon's Breath. She senses a solidity in the fog's depth, a swirling and gathering, and gazes transfixed as a real dragon materializes with majesty and fierceness. He soars through the fog, beating back the density with his powerful wings and looking for a way to escape. Sensing light above the fog, the dragon flies up and around, spiraling ever higher. Piercing through the grey-white cloudbank at last, the dragon disappears from view.

Ally waits for his return, staring at the point of his escape. He does not disappoint. The dragon tears through the cloudbank screeching with exaltation. He has found the sun beyond her sight. Where once he was a pale grey mirroring the stuff he was made of, now he is brilliant with many glistening colors and charged with the sun's vitality.

The dragon glides down in great swirling circles. His huge taloned feet skim the ocean waves as he lands on the stretch of beach beside her. Lowering his head, the dragon invites Ally to climb up on his back, and when she is secure, he soars swiftly upwards.

Seconds pass and together they burst through the clouds. He has taken her to the sun's fiery light, and she is an echo of his own glistening. Where once her hair was lackluster, now her long locks shine a brilliant red. Her plain white nightshirt has changed into a golden

gown. In her hand is a sword of brilliant silver. Ally and the dragon fly off on adventures, circling the world in pursuit of the next destination. She wishes she could live in this dream forever. She doesn't want to wake up to a powerless, pointless life. This is Ally's last thought before she falls deeper into sleep.

Ally's eyes pop open first thing in the morning before the alarm signals its wake-up call, feeling rested and energized. She stretches, feeling a new vitality in her body, and as she sits up on the edge of the bed flexing and pointing her feet, she begins to recall her dream. The vibrantly colored dragon is her spirit set free. Her transformation is inspiration allowed to blossom. With these realizations, she resolves to take steps towards a new life. She will leave her job and use her savings to travel the world. This first step will lead to the next as she allows her creative spirit the freedom it needs. Her life will become the dream. Feeling a jolt of energy, she jumps up from the bed ready to take the first step towards her new life. As for the silver sword, someday it will become the pen she uses to write about her adventures, inspiring others to follow their dreams.

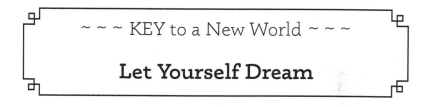

~ ~ ~ KEY to a New World ~ ~ ~

Let Yourself Dream

LIZARD BOY

PETER WAS ONE OF FOUR CHILDREN, THE youngest by many years. His older siblings had a fairly normal upbringing. When it was time for Peter to be ushered into this world, however, there were far too many family challenges for him to receive the guidance and support that a child requires. He was often left on his own. He grew to be a sensitive and kind child, but his sense of self was very small. Peter didn't quite know where he fit in the family puzzle and he didn't feel like he belonged. His life wasn't horrible, just lonely and withdrawn. Peter's story would have remained that way if not for two extraordinary events that gave him a larger sense of self and purpose.

The first event was a dream. He crawled into bed that night after a day of teasing by one of his older brothers. There was no one to tuck him in so he cried himself to sleep, thinking plaintively, "I wish I belonged."

Dreams came often to him, but this night's dream was special. It was very vivid and he knew, without a doubt, that he inhabited the body of a giant female lizard guarding her nest of smooth white eggs. She was bright green with a black stripe running down her back, and she was defending her nest with sharply clawed feet. He could feel, as a mother lizard, how fiercely protective she was of her future hatchlings.

When Peter awoke, he remembered the feeling, and he understood what we should all learn eventually— love and protect the child you are. That understanding gave him a solid footing. Now he had a foundation no one could take away.

The second event happened a few years later when the family decided to take a rare trip to the zoo. Everyone wanted to see their favorite animals: meerkats, gorillas, and polar bears. Peter especially wanted to see the reptiles, but the family never managed to find the exhibit. His brother pointed to the Amphibian Exhibit, but Peter knew better. "Amphibians are not reptiles," he protested.

Disappointed, Peter followed his family into the last exhibit. The penguins were amazing, but they didn't make up for the absence of the reptiles. He lagged behind as the family walked toward the zoo exit. Peter was looking down when he bumped into an older woman.

"Look where you're going, young man," she scolded.

Since he was a kind child, he looked up to apologize. And then he saw it—the Reptile Exhibit.

"Sorry," he said. "And thank you!" With excitement he ran for the door to a whole building devoted to reptiles.

It was warm inside, and he immediately relaxed from the shivering cold of the Penguin exhibit. How glorious! There were so many different kinds of lizards and snakes. He admired all of them. As Peter gazed through the glass displays, they emerged from their camouflaged perches and holes to greet him. Some had darting tongues, and others scampered quickly across the miniature landscapes. One rattlesnake looked directly at him. With unhinged jaws, its mouth opened in the widest yawn he had ever seen as if the rattlesnake would swallow him whole.

Peter felt like a magician. Every reptile acknowledged him, and he was sure that if freed from their glass cases, they would follow him anywhere. That thought made him smile with amusement. It also gave him an unexpected and deep sense of belonging.

"Why is this a campfire story?" you ask. Well, the story gives you another valuable key to navigate a new world.

We can grow up in the world feeling as if we don't belong, feeling alone. But on that day at the zoo, Peter realized that we all belong somewhere and that knowing you belong gives you the strength and courage to believe in yourself. The boy grew up to be a strong, self-assured man who was loved by many, and who shared his blessings with everyone.

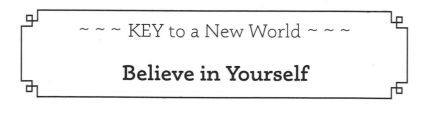

~ ~ ~ KEY to a New World ~ ~ ~

Believe in Yourself

LELLIE'S ADVENTURE

Y OU COULD SEE IT WHEN SHE WAS BARELY old enough to distinguish the world of shapes. She was startled and alarmed as objects and people came into focus. Sharp boundaries were too hard for her gentle soul. As time passed, she became accustomed to a world very different from her own, yet she never trusted it. People called her shy, but really she was terrified.

At home, Lellie lived in a world created to comfort her sensitive nature. Her home was surrounded by beautiful gardens all enclosed by a high wall and a single front gate. She never went beyond the wall, and her parents made sure that whatever she needed was brought to the house. Home was where she stayed, maintaining a measure of safety. Her birthdays passed, and Lellie matured into a beautiful, but timid, young girl. All was progressing well until the day her parents disappeared. She spent the first night anxiously awaiting their return. By morning she was in tears, overcome with uncertainty and fear. She wandered around her gardens to comfort and distract herself greeting the small animals and insects, her only friends. She begged the praying mantis on her porch, the rabbits in her garden, and the birds in the trees, "Please, please keep me safe."

A week passed and Lellie's parents were still absent. She had plenty of food in the house, but she had a special fondness for sweets. As the days went by, she fantasized about cookies and candy. On the seventh day there was a knock on the gate. It took an hour before she had enough courage to peek through the slats. Lellie spied a decorated bag filled with her favorite sweets sitting in front of the gate. Of course, she wondered how the bag arrived, but she was mostly petrified. Lellie had never opened the gate by herself. As she sat with her back against the gate, her mouth watered for the sweets she so badly wanted. A battle was brewing in her gentle being. Which was greater, the fear of stepping beyond her safe world, or the hunger for the yummy treats?

Fear, a large dark shape with arms and hands, reached to grasp and squeeze her. At the same time, Hunger in her screamed for the decorated bag. Louder and louder it screamed, demanding satisfaction. Finally, Fear dissolved into a puddle of water. Lellie stood up, opened the gate wide enough to grab the bag, and quickly shut it again. She turned to see the puddle of water before her. Looking back and forth between the puddle and the bag, she began to suspect she was stronger than her fear. Lellie experimented for the next week. Whenever she felt fear, she screamed and then watched as it dissolved into a puddle of water. With each success she treated herself to something sweet and delicious.

She began to feel courageous and with courage came determination. It was time to step through the gate. If only her parents were here to help. As Lellie remembered how comforting it was to stand between them, safe and protected, she heard a scratching on the gate. She opened it, and sitting before her was a large, beautiful black dog with brown markings on his face. His kind, soulful eyes were the eyes of her father. His soft fur was her mother's beautiful hair. She held the gate wide open as the dog walked in with great purpose. He surveyed the surroundings, taking full measure of the house, the gardens, and all the little creatures. Then he turned to look at Lellie and she knew he was there to protect her. She had called for that protection, and her call had been answered.

She wrapped her arms around the dog and whispered in his ear, "I shall call you Gabriel, Gabby for short. You are my guardian angel, and we will take a journey together."

🐞

Every good journey begins with knowing your travel companion. Every day, Lellie walked Gabby around the gardens introducing him to life within the walls. All the small animals, birds, and insects greeted Gabby warily at first, but in time they came to accept him. He was quite the prince in her world, keeping everything in perfect order. He was trusted and respected by all. Lellie dearly loved Gabby, and as time passed, they developed a deep knowing of each other and mutual communication.

Gabby had a plan, and his first challenge was getting Lellie out the garden gate. He stood by the gate barking, and when she finally opened it, thinking that he wanted out, he pulled her right along. Before she knew it, she was standing outside her secure wall. Trusting Gabby, she followed as he trotted purposefully around the block. How wonderful to be so free, she thought. After many excursions outside her wall, Lellie gained some real confidence.

There came a day when Lellie and Gabby had the same thought. It was time for a longer journey. So they closed up the house, bid farewell to all the creatures, and locked the gate. Dog and girl started the journey they were meant to take together. Lellie always felt secure with Gabby by her side.

After many weeks, they came to a river blocking their path. Gabby barked and a small boat magically appeared on the bank. They climbed in the boat and floated down the river in an entirely new direction. The pace of the water quickened and soon the boat's momentum lost all control. Faster and faster the boat sped, passing grassy banks, flowers, and trees. Up ahead, the river dropped off into a cascading waterfall. Unable to stop the boat, the two went over the falls and down to a very different world. The boat emerged from drenching mists and was soon floating serenely on calmer waters. The riverbanks were rocky and barren. Cliffs on either side held the promise of hidden caves. Lellie and Gabby, eager to explore, pulled the boat up to the shore.

Before them was a very promising cave, and as they approached the opening, an old hermit emerged. He was dressed in long robes and carried a tall staff. "Where do you go?" he asked looking directly at Gabby. After a moment, the old man nodded, understanding that the destination would be a truth revealed. The hermit looked at Lellie and said, "If you are worthy, you will see the wild horses." He pointed to a path through a cleft in the cliffs.

Lellie and Gabby continued their journey along the path and eventually came to a crystal blue lake amid a landscape washed with brilliant hues of yellows, oranges, and reds. Lellie settled on a nearby rock with an overview of the magical lake. Gabby sat alert beside her. Just then, a canoe appeared in the distance with one figure paddling and the old hermit standing on the bow. He pointed behind Lellie. When she turned in the direction the hermit was pointing, she saw a herd of wild horses galloping towards her. There were so many, all with different colors, flowing manes, and lashing tails. As they came closer, they veered around, galloping in a large circle enclosing the girl and her dog. They galloped with flare and joy, freedom and purpose.

The horses called out to Lellie, "For you, we have three gifts. The first is the gift of family. You will always be part of all who have come before you and all who follow. You and family are bonded together as one just as we gallop and speak as one."

The horses began to slow their pace. What was once a single whirling unit, transformed into a choreography of dancing horses as they playfully kicked up their hooves in many blended rhythms.

With one voice they sang, "The second is the gift of dance. You will always know the expression of movement and joy."

Now the horses began to circle again. One after the other, their hooves left the ground, and in a single line, they flew up into the sky circling off towards the horizon. As they flew, the horses called down to Lellie, "The third gift is knowing that there is something much greater than yourself, and you will know this great spirit as your true home. You will always be loved and protected by that which binds us all together." And with the giving of the last gift they were gone.

Lellie gazed at the vast sky and then down into Gabby's soulful eyes. This had been his plan all along. Now she knew a truth greater than any fear. Together they would forge a new path back home.

~ ~ ~ KEY to a New World ~ ~ ~

Transform Your Fear

FATHER OF LIGHT, DAUGHTER OF THE VOID

THE VILLAGE STOOD AT A CROSSROADS BACKED up to the eastern slopes of the mountains, gateway to the plains. It had been home to its founding families for generations, and life in the village was protected from the quickening pace of the cities. Pueblo ancestors had built a ceremonial Kiva far from the homes that dotted the hills and valleys. It was a round underground room with a small opening in its roof and a log ladder leading down to a quiet interior. Remains of a small fire pit held secrets of countless ceremonies, and a diagonal shaft to its side allowed sacred smoke to escape. Centuries ago, the Kiva was home to a society of men bound together to protect the knowledge of their people and to guard the intent and history of its sacred brotherhood. The Kiva had been abandoned and forgotten until it was rediscovered by the village's most unusual man.

Don Jose was unschooled, but he had an instinctive knowledge of mystical things and a powerful insight that transcended the physical world. Discovering the Kiva awakened those gifts in an extraordinary way and gave his life a new purpose. Ordinary villagers feared Don Jose's premonitions and perceptions, and he lived a solitary life with no wife or family. But time was passing, and the man was aging. He needed to find an apprentice to take his place. Every day he walked to his secret Kiva and relit the fire pit. Then he prayed for the gift of someone he could pass his knowledge on to.

Back in the village, Don Jose looked intently at all the boys and young men, but he never found a suitable apprentice. He was losing all hope, when one day a very small girl appeared on his doorstep. He thought she must be lost so he took her by the hand and asked each villager if they knew where she belonged. No one had ever seen her before and by nightfall Don Jose realized that she must be the answer to his prayers. He took her back to his home, and she became his beloved daughter.

Don Jose had never considered a girl as his apprentice, but she exhibited so much intelligence and eagerness to learn that he was forced to abandon his preconceptions. He took her on daily walks as he taught her about the land, the animals, and the spirit present in all things. The villagers thought the girl was a little strange, and they didn't trust her quick intelligence. But they left her alone and that suited Don Jose. He would often ask her to describe what she saw as they walked, and when it became clear that she also could see beyond the physical world, he knew that it was time to introduce her to the Kiva.

Father and daughter walked under a bright sun to the secret Kiva, her eyes widening as he carried her down the log ladder. It was cool in the underground room, a welcome relief from the summer heat. The girl let go of Don Jose's hand to examine the fire pit, and as she listened for its secrets, he quickly climbed the ladder, pulled it up, and closed the roof hatch. She was terrified to be suddenly immersed in darkness. She whimpered for her father, but he waited for her silence.

After a time she was quiet, and when he sensed a calmness, he called down to her, "If you want to leave you must follow the light." She peered around the dark Kiva and saw a glimmer of light coming through the smoke shaft. "Follow the light, Daughter," he called out again and she crawled up and out of the shaft just like the sacred smoke from the fire pit.

He watched the shaft opening from above as her little head popped out, and when she fully emerged, he expected her to run with relief into his arms. Instead, she stood silently by the shaft opening, and he knew at once that she had glimpsed a profound secret. The girl was very quiet on the way home, and as Don Jose held her hand, he felt a new depth to her being.

"You have met The Void, Daughter," he explained with care. "It is the birthplace of creation where everything begins. Out of the darkness the light emerges." That evening at home, her first words were to ask to visit the Kiva again.

They went to the Kiva many times in the remaining years they had together. Sometimes, they sat around the fire pit and watched the flames dance. Other times, they sat together in complete darkness feeling the charged emptiness. Don Jose taught her all he knew, and when he took his last breath, he did so with the serenity that destiny had been fulfilled. The legacy of his knowledge would continue through future generations of teachers and apprentices.

As the Daughter said her last goodbye to her father, she heard a soft whinny and looked up to see a white horse through the window. By the time she opened the door, the horse had galloped to the crest of the nearby hill. He reared up on his back legs, front hooves pawing the air, and galloped off towards the Kiva. She followed, yearning for the peace the Kiva could offer. As she sat in the darkness allowing herself to feel the emptiness, she began to know the great Void where all is created and all returns. Surrendering to this experience, she became aware of a presence as soft as a breath of air, and she knew it was the spirit of her father. Gently, she led him to the light shining down the shaft. His spirit, sensing light, floated up the shaft to the heavens above. As the years passed, Don Jose's daughter made an effort to connect with the villagers. She was kind and helpful in their times of need, and they grew to trust and love her. She even found several apprentices to continue the stream of knowledge, each enhancing the flow with their own unique gifts. Many times she repeated the precious service in the Kiva for all whose earthly time had ended, guiding each presence in The Void towards the light.

When her own time arrived, her spirit already knew the way. She floated toward a light that differentiated into the many memories of all she had known. Many arms reached out to welcome and embrace her, and when her spirit was fully joined to all, their light became one.

~ ~ ~ KEY to a New World ~ ~ ~

Follow The Light

In His Brother's Footsteps

J ACK'S FIRST MEMORY WAS OF LYING IN HIS
playpen, eyes as big as saucers. His older brother
was running in circles around the mini prison, arms
outstretched, singing, "If I had the wings of an angel."
Bob loved anything to do with flying, and he already
knew he wanted to be a pilot when he grew up. A few
years later, the brothers were flying around the room
together singing at the top of their voices with an added
verse, "Over these prison walls I would fly!" Bob was a
dreamer and a bit of a daredevil. Even though Jack was
more sensible and down to earth, he was willing to follow his brother's lead. They grew to rely on each other,
and there was much love and admiration between the
two.

When the world went crazy with war, it was every
young man's dream to defend his country. Bob enlisted
in the Army Air Core and by 1941 he was a pilot flying
cargo ships over the mountains between India and
China. Letters home described exotic places and daring missions; Jack could hardly wait to follow. Then the
letters stopped, and after months without a word, Bob's

plane was listed as missing in action, lost somewhere in the mountains.

For Jack, determination and hope overshadowed uncertainty and fear. As soon as he was old enough, he too would also enlist and train as a pilot. It would be his mission to find his brother. But before his mission could be accomplished, the war ended and Jack was left with a harsh reality. His brother was gone, and he had no feasible way to find him. Determination melted away and hope evaporated. What was left was too painful to bear. Jack buried the grief deep within his heart, locked away and never fully felt. He lived his life with gusto but without emotional richness and tenderness.

Many years later, Jack received a letter. A man and his guide had found the wreckage of Bob's plane while they were trekking in the mountains. They traced the crew manifest from the plane's still visible serial number and family members were contacted. Jack was offered the opportunity to join a second trek, but his first reaction was to reject the offer. After all, it was a long time ago and it didn't matter anymore. Bob, as the pilot, must have made a mistake, he reasoned. But then he felt a nudge from his heart, and he remembered the times he shared with his brother. The more he remembered, the more his heart opened. There was no way to deny what was now obvious: he must go!

Jack landed in a city in northeast India on the same airfield where his brother had been stationed. From there, a bumpy Jeep ride took him into the foothills of the Himalayas where he met two men, the original trekker and the guide native to the area of the crash site. They drove as far as the terrain allowed, and then they trekked on foot through foothill passes and hidden valleys. Eventually, they came to the crash site on the side of a mountain.

What on earth had happened? Jack wondered. The mountains weren't particularly high. Bob had an excellent reputation as a responsible pilot. What mistake could he have made? Walking up to a piece of wreckage, part of one of the engines, Jack knelt down and bowed his head. In a flash of insight, he saw the plane take off in questionable weather. Flying through a bank of clouds, it crashed against the side of the mountain. The demands of war must not have allowed for a thorough safety check of the plane and its failing instrument panel. Jack realized that Bob had done his best with what he had to work with: an unreliable plane, fickle weather, and an inexperienced skeleton crew of young men. The realization flooded Jack's mind and made its way into the depths of his heart. His grief released in the song that he and his brother shared so often.

"If I had the wings of an angel, over these prison walls I would fly!" he sang. Nearby mountains echoed his song and, as he looked up, he noticed the guide watching with a curious expression. Jack quickly stood to examine the rest of the wreckage, sheepish that his moment of emotion had been witnessed. The guide touched Jack's shoulder gently and then pointed to a valley north of the mountain.

The three men started towards the valley and after a few hours arrived at the guide's village. Strangers were seldom seen in the village and curious people lined the main road. Jack looked around and shook his head to dismiss an overwhelming sense that something reminiscent of his brother appeared in the small gathered groups. His imagination must be playing tricks. The guide took him to the center of the village, where all followed. Then the guide urged Jack to sing again. It must be the echo, Jack thought. They want to hear the echo. He obliged and sang the first verse with a booming voice now let loose from his once locked heart.

"If I had the wings of an angel," he sang. Jack paused for a few seconds to give the echo a chance to dance between the mountains. But before he could sing the second verse the whole village erupted with, "Over these prison walls I would fly!" Jack was dumbfounded. How did they know, halfway around the world, this snippet of a song he and his brother sang decades ago?

The excited villagers gathered around Jack creating quite a commotion. The guide stepped forward, motioned the crowd to silence, and began the story. Years ago the village witnessed a plane crash in the mountains. A group was assembled to look for survivors. They brought a seriously injured pilot back to the village to heal. Bob's fragile hold on life was tenuous as he drifted in and out of consciousness.

Many times the village healers witnessed an inspiration of breath and the glimmer of a smile as they heard a whisper of a song on his lips. What they didn't know was that, in those moments, Bob was reliving the times the brothers played pilots together, soaring through the air, and finally revisiting the first time he ran circles around the playpen. The healers didn't understand the language of the song but they memorized it, thinking it could be the magic Bob needed. Each time the healers sang the song, more villagers gathered around, adding their voices to the call for life. But the angels heard the call for freedom and finally lifted Bob to heaven on their wings. Jack had truly followed in his brother's footsteps to this village and someday he too would sing their song one last time, rejoining his brother forever.

~ ~ ~ KEY to a New World ~ ~ ~

Open Your Heart

THE GARDEN

T HERE IS A SPECIAL GARDEN ON A PARTICU-
lar street in the Candlelight District of the city.
It grows in front of a gated wall where all can view its
progress as they pass. Most pass in their cars, too intent
on their destination to notice much else. Sometimes, a
car will slow and the garden will be enjoyed for a brief
moment. A few people walk by. They have more time to
notice the changes from day to day, season to season.

In January all is covered with a quiet blanket of snow.
As driveways and sidewalks are cleared, the garden
receives the extra bounty of the future melt. A mountain landscape is sculpted. Hidden valleys and taller
peaks form a mini panorama of the Sangre De Cristo
Mountains. All is still on the surface, but underneath a
whole world begins to awaken.

February encourages the melt with its ever so slight
warming and the ground is often wet and soggy. Tiny
sprouts poke their green blades through the earth's surface. The bulbs are the first to emerge. Hyacinth and
daffodils race to see who will bloom first. The tulips
bide their time. This is an exceptional year for the daffodils. Many expectant stems spring up surrounded by
their entourage of bladelike leaves.

March brings an explosion of yellow trumpets and little bunches of purple, pink, and white hyacinths, calling out to the first arriving bees. They stand resolute through the early spring weather, tolerating an occasional dusting of snow or dip in temperature.

Listen closely to their conversations. This year feels different. There is less rush and the people are quiet.

"Finally," the flowers say, "more will pay attention to our beauty, our story, our rhythm." This observation is worth sharing with their garden mates, and they send the news down through their bulbs and roots. Fungi pick up the message and telegraph it to the sleepy garden community.

"Be ready," the message calls, "this year is like no other and the world needs your gifts."

Mother Earth is satisfied that the message has been heard as she provides the elements needed to meet the healing call. The daffodils and hyacinths are excited and their colors intensify. They can hardly wait to be joined in succession by the multi-colored tulips, the majestic irises, the giant red poppies, the stunning roses, the fragrant lavender spears, the spiritual salvia, the medicinal yarrow, the long-stemmed daisies, the Russian sage and the butterfly bush with its life-giving blossoms. Each will have its time to explode upon the scene, in all their various stages, creating a healing garden. This is their message.

"Slow down and drop into the rhythm of Mother Earth. She holds the knowledge and wisdom of all who have come before you. Let her gardens embrace you with their healing hues and gentle smells. Relax, trust, and surrender to a force greater than yourself."

The first to hear the message is the one who tends the garden. She has always known this garden loves to be shared, but now the need is more immediate. She places a small stool in the garden as an invitation to be part of this miracle of nature. "Come and sit awhile and be part of this vibrant, abundant life. Surround yourself with greenery, flowers, bees, moths, butterflies, and birds. Listen for the message that's especially for you."

~ ~ ~ KEY to a New World ~ ~ ~

Allow The Miracle Of Life

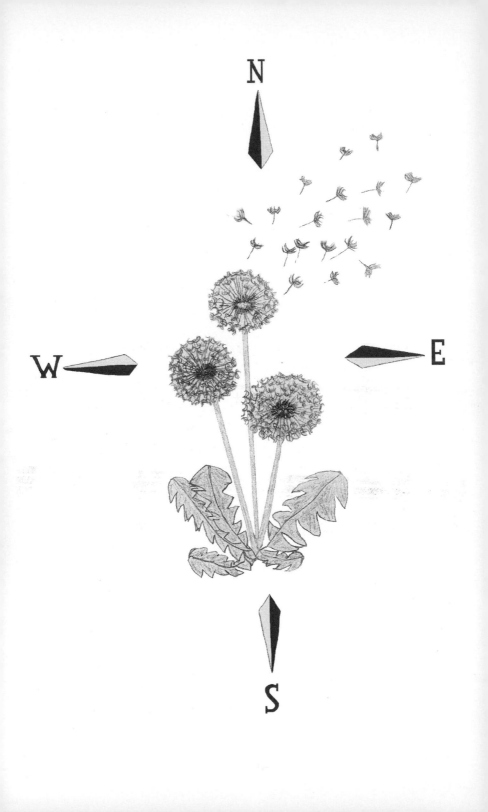

DANDELIONS

ONCE THERE WAS A YOUNG GIRL WHO LOVED to explore the fields behind her family's home. As winter turned to spring, she searched for the first green sprouts. The dandelion was her favorite plant, and when they turned the fields a brilliant yellow, she liked to pretend that a thousand little suns warmed the early spring chill. As yellow flowers changed to puffy white spheres, she ran through the fields, releasing the tiny parachutes into the spring winds. The girl loved to imagine where these airborne seeds would land and vowed that someday she too would freely give herself up to the wind.

This sense of freedom was a defining attribute as the girl grew to be an independent young woman. When she did marry, it was to a husband who appreciated and shared this quality. On their wedding night they made a pact to visit the four corners of the world. But first, they would start their life together in the center of the world. They built a home, which would be their anchor, a place they could always return to. It was an ample home to accommodate the large family they hoped to have, and it was surrounded by fields of dandelions.

When all was complete, they looked to the rising sun in the East and decided this would be their first destination. They joined a caravan to an exotic land of silk and spices, following the flight of eagles. The smells, colors, and tastes of the place were all illuminated by the golden light of the rising sun. The land was so seductive that they lingered longer than they realized. Their first son was born bathed in the glowing light of new beginnings. The new Mother took a lock of her first son's hair and buried it in a treasure box so that the East would always remember him. Then they returned home to the center of the world and lived happily as their new son grew strong and sturdy. He loved the feel of the dirt beneath his feet and his connection to the Earth was a reminder of how life begins.

When it was time to travel again, they looked to the South. This time fiery white stallions took them to a beautiful oasis deep in the desert. Their first daughter was born in this land of passion and creativity. The Mother took a lock of her first daughter's hair and buried it in another treasure box so the South would always recognize its own. They returned home and lived happily as their first daughter grew full of fire and energy, a reminder of what it is that fuels life.

The next journey took them to the West. They traveled across the ocean on a ship accompanied by dolphins to a land surrounded by water. The constant movement of the crashing waves against the shore evoked deep emotions and the second son was born with a depth of feeling. Once again, the Mother buried a lock of her son's hair in a treasure box so the West would always call to his heart. Back home, their second son grew to be kind and heartfelt.

Their last journey was to the North, where the land slept under a blanket of snow. They traveled on sleds pulled by dogs until they came to a village. Their

second daughter was born in a land that encouraged thoughtfulness and wisdom where all turned inward to contemplate the great journey of life. One last time, the Mother buried a lock of her daughter's hair in a treasure box deep in the snow so that the North would always recognize this child, who would grow to be a wise sage.

Back home, the family lived happily for many years. The four children grew up playing in the fields of dandelions. They all loved the flying seeds, and when each was old enough, they followed the little parachutes to the directions and lands that they were born to. East, South, West, and North remembered their own, and the four siblings settled in their respective lands.

Many years later there was trouble in the center of the world. The Earth was sick and the dandelions were gone. The parents called to their family to return home and help with the healing. Each brought their treasure box back to the center of the world, and the four boxes were buried in the dandelion fields. They also brought the gifts of the Four Directions of East, South, West and North that they each embodied.

From the East came new beginnings. From the South came fire and passion. From the West came fullness and heartfelt feeling. From the North came wisdom. These realized gifts brought a great healing to the center of the world and the dandelions returned to their cycle of life reminding all to emerge, grow, and finally take flight to every corner of the world. Gather all that the Four Directions have to offer and when needed, return with your gifts to the center.

~ ~ ~ KEY to a New World ~ ~ ~

Expand Your Horizons

LITTLE BA

PART ONE

T SILLAH WAS THE YOUNGEST IN A VERY
large family living on the edge of poverty. Since
she was a girl and not old enough to be useful, her value
lay in what she could be bartered for. So, as was the cus-
tom in Egypt, her parents promised her to the local temple to train as an initiate. She didn't realize it then, but
she was about to embark on the journey of a lifetime.

Tsillah was timid by nature and small for her age.
Although she was apprehensive of the coming change,
there was not much she would miss about her early
years. She was often forgotten, last to receive food or a
warm blanket on a cold night. At least the temple would
provide for her basic needs, and although her days
would be filled with work and study, it would be good to
feel useful for once.

On the day Tsillah left for the temple, her family
lined up to say goodbye. They would receive special
favors from the local authorities for her barter and the

parents thought it only right that the other children recognize her service. A pat on the head from her father and a kiss on the cheek from her mother was her last contact with the family. Then Tsillah turned her back on the only home she had known.

Two hooded and silent initiates escorted Tsillah down dusty streets. Her little body trembled with fear as the temple loomed ahead at the end of a wide causeway. Seven enormous steps, each as wide as the pyramid shaped structure itself, led up to a large platform used for various temple functions. A doorway flanked by two large columns stood at the back of the platform. Above the doorway, carved in relief, were figures of the initiates engaging in various temple functions. Among the human figures were little cats carved in many poses, some stately, some playful, and some curled up sleeping. Tsillah gazed at the carvings thoughtfully. The cats she had known were wild, only good for keeping the mice under control. These cats seemed to be part of everyday life. She climbed the steps to the platform, accompanied by the initiates. At the top she turned to face the dusty city and say her goodbyes. Then, Tsillah crossed the wide platform, entered through the doorway, and began a new chapter in her young life.

The first room she entered was a vast ceremonial chamber with rows of columns on either side. Three reflecting pools were encircled by stone ledges wide enough to sit on while one peered down into still water. Little oil lamps floated on the water and larger wall torches provided a silent light.

The initiates led her past the pools and along the columns on the right side to a hallway lined with many doors. They stopped in front of one open door and motioned her into the small room. Tsillah entered and the wooden door closed behind her. Her own sleeping pallet lay against the wall on one side of the room. Above the head of the pallet was a small opening to let in the light of the outside world.

Tsillah stood on the pallet and looked out the little window. Not much to see, just another dusty street. She imagined that each of the hallway rooms had a window, and that from the street, one would look at the long row of openings and wonder about the lives of those behind the pyramid walls.

It wasn't long before she heard a soft knock and the wooden door opened slightly to reveal a long line of girls in the hallway. She gingerly slipped into place in the line. The line led through an opening at the back of the hallway where the girls found themselves in a large bathhouse with washing pools and spigots of running water. They washed themselves from head to toe, and attendants dressed them in white shifts and gave them sandals woven from river grasses. After their baths, the girls were led to an adjoining room where they sat at long tables and ate an ample meal. Tsillah was so immersed in these simple luxuries that she had not taken measure of the girls around her. She was used to feeling suspicious of the intentions of others and now she looked warily from girl to girl assessing any danger. Everyone kept to herself; they all felt a little unsure.

When the clatter of the meal was finally quieted down, an older, austere woman stood up and motioned for the girls to follow. They walked through another opening and down the hallway on the opposite side of the pyramid into the great chamber with the three pools. They had gone around in a full circle arriving back where they had started. Tsillah would make this circle many times in her years at the temple. Sometime counterclockwise, sometimes clockwise, the circle dictated a slow, steady rhythm conducive to silence and deep thought.

The woman motioned the girls to find a seat around the three pools. Shyly, they looked around, never daring to meet anyone's eyes. She let them sit in silence for a long time, and when busy minds were finally still, she rose to speak.

"I am Tasherit, the High Priestess of this temple and your teacher. This has been your first lesson. Nothing will be taught until minds are quiet. We practice silence, and you will learn your lessons as mind connects to mind. It is a language full of nuances far richer than the spoken word. Listen inwardly and you will know what is asked of you." Then she walked across the great chamber towards the hallway. The girls looked at one another, unsure what to do. Finally, they rose from their seats and followed the High Priestess to their sleeping rooms without a word spoken.

The days at the temple were filled with the quiet rhythm of bathing, eating, learning, and sleeping—there was never a wasted moment. The girls became adept at telepathy, the language of mind to mind. They learned to care for the temple and themselves with reverence, to prepare healing foods and medicinal drinks, and to gaze into the reflecting pools looking for inner truths.

Then one day, the High Priestess surprised them with the strong clear sound of a musical tone—the study of the arts began that day. The girls learned to sing and play flutes, cymbals, and little stringed harps. They learned to dance with flowing, sweeping movements to calm a frenzied nervous system.

Preparation began for a presentation on the temple platform. The day of the performance was the first time the girls had left the safety of the pyramid walls in many months. Nonetheless, they were unfazed by the noisy world outside their walls as they performed with skill and quiet grace. The High Priestess was satisfied with their progress and let it be known there would be a reward. Actually, this was the next step in their education. The girls were ready to be introduced to their guides. Each would receive her very own cat.

PART TWO

Cat was once worshipped as one of the many gods and goddesses in Egypt. When Tsillah first arrived, the temple was devoted to the cat. But this was the time of Pharaoh Amenhotep IV, and divinely inspired, he declared there to be only one God, and that God was represented by the splendor of the sun. The High Priestess knew a change must be made as she contemplated how her life's work could transition into something supportive of this new belief. She requested an audience with Pharaoh to plead her case.

When the day arrived, Tasherit dressed carefully and humbly. The elegant costume and painted face of a priestess were no longer appropriate. She must play the part of a wise teacher and convince the man before her that the initiates could facilitate the connection to the one God. She explained to the Pharaoh that the cat was not a god, but instead, a servant who guarded the doorway to the subconscious mind. When that doorway was carefully opened, a true connection to the one God could be established. Pharaoh listened. He was willing to let this teacher transform the temple into a school for initiates who could help his people with a new way of understanding. So just before the girls were rewarded with their own cat, subtle changes were implemented.

Now girl and cat would form a partnership in their service to this one God.

On the day a large group of cats arrived at the school, Tasherit, the Teacher, sat among the cats to communicate their newly defined responsibilities. Each cat had a serious duty as guide and companion. Once Teacher was satisfied that they each understood their mission, she ordered the felines to take a seat around the three reflecting pools.

There were twenty cats of all different sizes and colors. As they jumped up to their positions, the cats reflected on their task. They would introduce each girl to the doorway of her own subconscious—each cat was the keeper of one of the girl's doorways. When all was safe, each girl would step through her own doorway into a vast, connected universe that held the secrets of past, present, and future. In this universe would be access to knowledge, but more importantly, it would be where each girl would develop her own connection to the one God.

The girls entered the great ceremonial chamber and stood in a tightly clustered group amazed to see the cats in various positions around the pools. Each cat was meant to attract the girl who most resonated with what it projected. At Teacher's bidding, each girl drew near to her perfect cat. Tsillah, the most timid of all the girls, was the last to step forward. She had to search for the remaining cat, and as she walked around the pools, she saw how perfectly each cat matched its companion. Finally, Tsillah found the last cat, the smallest and most delicate of all. She sat next to her cat and stroked its multi-colored fur; they bonded instantly.

Tsillah and her cat spent the first week learning how to communicate without words. It was important to develop a telepathic connection, as much work would be done in the dream state. The girls were allowed to name their cats, and they chose many grand and beautiful names. Tsillah, who was beginning to grasp the important purpose of the cats as guides for a soul's journey, named her cat Little Ba. Ba was the Egyptian word for soul and her cat was the smallest of all. Little Ba loved the name and responded with pleasure whenever called.

Weeks went by swiftly and playfully. The cats slept on pillows at the heads of the sleeping pallets so that they could join with their companions in the dreamworld. They were always present with their girls whether they were awake, meditating, or sleeping. Once the strong bonds between the girls and the cats were developed, it was time for the next step.

That night, as she slept, Little Ba sat inside the open doorway to Tsillah's subconscious, waiting patiently for dreamtime. As she dreamt, Tsillah walked toward the doorway with apprehension, each step filled with fear. Little Ba sent reassuring thoughts, but Tsillah's fear was too great. Ominous black clouds swirled around the doorway as her fear created imaginary ghosts and demons. Little Ba had no choice but to slam the door shut in order to keep these unwelcome figments out of the sacred space. Tsillah woke startled from her frightful dream. Little Ba was nowhere to be seen, shut away from Tsillah's earthly life.

Tsillah failed this important test, overcome by her own fear. She was no longer allowed to train as an initiate and spent the rest of her days as an attendant serving the school and the other girls. Fortunately, Little Ba, separated from Tsillah by the closed doorway, was given the chance to rectify the disappointing failure. The cat would have nine lives to find the soul who was Tsillah and finish what was started. Throughout the centuries, the two souls were born again and again but never at the same time. The soul who was Tsillah lived lifetimes learning love and kindness, strength and grace, wisdom and fearlessness, as all souls do. Little Ba spent eight life-times looking for Tsillah. The cat only had one life left.

PART THREE

The man was getting used to being alone. His favorite black kitty had died a year ago, and he had not thought about another companion. But, as he was reading the Sunday paper, he came across an ad for the animal shelter. He thought he might go and check it out just for something to do. The man arrived before the doors were opened and noticed some large windows on the side of the building, so he decided to take a peek.

Inside, were wide windowsills where the cats could walk their length from room to room. A handsome multi-colored cat sat in the first window waiting for someone special. As the man walked past each window, a cat followed him along the sills. This caught his attention. When the doors opened, he asked to see the cat that was so determined to be noticed. An hour later he was home with his new companion. The man named the cat KitKit, and Little Ba did not mind this new name one bit.

This was Little Ba's last life, the ninth. The cat didn't know where the soul of Tsillah was, but something about this man was intriguing. He was a hypnotherapy teacher who knew about the subconscious. Little Ba was content to sleep next to him at night and traveled through his doorway into the great expanse of the universe. Sometimes, Little Ba would sit by Tsillah's closed doorway, and the man would follow in his dreams. Maybe there was a chance that he would find the soul of Tsillah.

Then, one day the man brought a woman home, someone who had graduated from his school. Little Ba thought this might be the soul of Tsillah, but there would need to be a signal. So, the cat joined with this possible long-lost companion and waited patiently.

One day, nestled in the woman's loving arms, the cat heard the magic words, "I love you Little Ba." The woman had no idea how this name came to her but it felt right. It was undeniable. Little Ba had found the soul of Tsillah and now the cat could correct the ancient failure.

The first thing to address was the old fear. So, one night, as the woman slept, Little Ba conjured a gremlin and placed it on the woman's back. The soul of Tsillah lost no time in dealing with this figment. She had spent lifetimes developing the courage to deal with fear. With her dream body, she stood up, faced the gremlin, and hissed at it. The gremlin melted away into the nothingness that it was. Little Ba was satisfied that this test was handled decisively so she started sleeping with the woman at night, joining her in dreamtime.

Little Ba once again sat at the open doorway to the great universe, and this time the soul of Tsillah walked through unafraid. The woman was amazed as she saw the past, present, and future. All the knowledge of the universe was there, but it was the direct connection to the one God that made lifetimes of trial, error, and sometimes success, all worth the soul's journey. Together the cat and the girl walked back through the door and gently closed it.

Little Ba lay curled up purring quietly, satisfied that the ninth life fulfilled the promise of a bond begun centuries ago. The woman woke gently from the dream with a soul purpose to embody and share what new possibilities now lay open. Many times they would travel through the doorway together as the woman listened closely for revealed secrets. The journey that began in ancient Egypt could finally be realized.

~ ~ ~ KEY to a New World ~ ~ ~

Listen For Your Purpose

THE BUTTERFLY

ELENI HURRIED DOWN THE STAIRS FROM the upper flat. The library next door to her home was opening soon, and she wanted to be the first one through the doors. She didn't have much time because it was Saturday and that meant chores and house cleaning. An arm full of newly checked out books stacked on her desk would be something to look forward to. Eleni was a very smart girl, and the library was the only place to quench her thirst for knowledge. She wanted to know about everything, and anything could spark her interest.

It was a beautiful spring afternoon by the time Eleni had finally finished her chores. The sun had burned through the morning fog, and her younger siblings were eager to play outside. She had no desire for their silly games, but Papa called to his children to come and see the backyard apricot tree. It was in full bloom and butterflies swarmed around its delicate flowers. The children ran through the kitchen, out the back door, and down the back stairs to the yard. Eleni groaned as she tore herself from her books and reluctantly followed.

"Interesting. It's pretty," she grudgingly admitted to no one in particular. Papa shook his head and said, "Eleni, you must see with your heart as well as your head." She listened to her father but she wasn't sure what he meant. She preferred the clarity of her books.

The next day Eleni visited the library and was surprised to see an exhibit of butterflies mounted and framed to show off their exquisite diversity. The beautiful colors and variations of pattern caught her eye and gave her an idea. The girl ran home—no books in her arms this time—to collect the money she had saved. A visit to the hobby store produced what she needed to make her own display. Now all she needed was the perfect specimen.

Eleni waited patiently next to the apricot tree until she spied the largest, most beautiful butterfly. Adeptly, she squeezed the wings between her fingers as the butterfly froze in her grasp. When she was ready to arrange this magnificent specimen, she took a long needle from her sewing kit and pierced through the butterfly's body pinning it to the display. Its wings fluttered slightly and then it froze again. Eleni was proud of what she had accomplished. Her butterfly was just as beautiful as the specimens in the library. She placed the framed trophy on her desk against the wall so she could glance at it as she read.

The next day, when Papa saw the butterfly display, he shook his head. "Eleni, what have you done to this beauty?" As he walked away, she glanced at the butterfly and its wings shuddered ever so slightly. She expected to make her Papa proud but he was only saddened by her accomplishment. Now she felt a little ashamed, so she hid the display from sight in her desk's top drawer.

Eleni forgot about the butterfly for a week. She buried the little bit of shame she felt deep in her heart and continued with her reading. When she did peek at the butterfly again, she was surprised to see the wings shudder. Maybe it was still alive! Eleni quickly unpinned it and ran down the back stairs to the apricot tree. She placed the butterfly on her wrist flicking it up to encourage a flight of freedom. But the butterfly dropped to the ground, all life seemingly gone.

Eleni knelt down to look at the butterfly. She had caused its suffering, and she was sorry. Papa watched from the kitchen window as she slowly made her way upstairs. The girl stood before him, her head hanging down.

"I'm sorry, Papa," she said.

He patted her head and said, "You have learned that we must have empathy for all living things."

Eleni went back to her reading but all was not completely well. She felt a deep discomfort she couldn't explain and was irritable and a little cranky. Papa watched for a week, understanding that his eldest daughter carried a burden.

On the following Sunday Papa took the family to the park. He instructed the children to walk quietly as they followed him to a special grove of trees. At the count of three, they all clapped hands as loudly as they could. The trees came to life with thousands of startled butterflies taking flight. Eleni was delighted, and as her outstretched arm reached toward the magnificent sight, a beautiful butterfly landed on her wrist.

Her heart swelled and opened as she exclaimed, "You are my butterfly! You have come back to me!" Then tears filled her eyes as she remembered the suffering she had caused. Her head hung down, and she was ashamed to look at her butterfly.

"I'm sorry," she said.

"I forgive you," the butterfly replied. Surprised, Eleni looked up with tear filled eyes. "But you must forgive yourself," continued the butterfly. Release the shame buried in your heart and you will have peace." "How do I do that?" Eleni asked. "You must realize that you stand surrounded by creation; you are no more and no less important than any other creature," the butterfly answered, flying away.

Eleni turned to look at Papa. He was watching and listening to everything. He wrapped his arms around her as she laid her head on his heart.

"Find the compassion for all creation by valuing all life as well as your own," Papa explained. "Then you can live a proud life and still have humility. This is a hard lesson for one so young to understand. Most of us take a lifetime to come to this realization. Learn this lesson now and live your life free from the burden of guilt. As for the shame, give it to the butterflies. They will take it to the heavens where all will be transformed into love."

That is exactly what Eleni did. She thought about her butterfly every day, and when she felt her heart swell and open, she let herself float down into a place of deep peace. There, surrounded by butterflies, she knew that compassion and forgiveness belonged to everyone. She carried that knowing for the rest of her life.

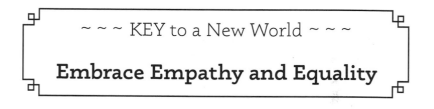

~ ~ ~ KEY to a New World ~ ~ ~

Embrace Empathy and Equality

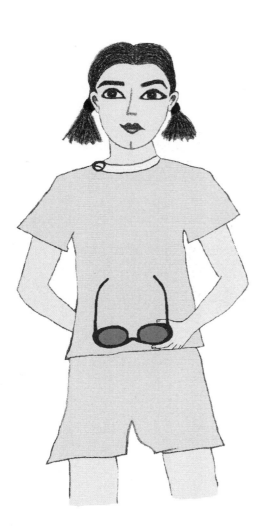

THE ROSE COLORED GLASSES

MAMA WAS BUSY COOKING, AND AS USUAL, Kiki got in the way trying to help. She adored her mother and would do anything for a soft, loving word. But Mama was a realist and too busy with the responsibilities of life. She was strict and her words were often stern. So that morning in the kitchen, Mama shooed Kiki away and told her to play somewhere else. This didn't discourage Kiki; she simply did everything her mother said, no questions asked.

Kiki knew exactly where she would go to play. She skipped, somewhat awkwardly, out of the kitchen, up the stairs, and down the long hallway directly to Mama's beautiful sunlit room. She loved this room with its large windows that looked down on the street and the wonderful rug covering most of the floor. It was decorated with large pink roses that Kiki liked to pretend were homes for her paper dolls. This was what she intended to play as she opened the door to Mama's large closet to retrieve her book of paper dolls. But Mama had moved the book in one of her cleaning frenzies, and Kiki had to search for its new location. The closet was large, with a window to let in light and fresh air. Kiki looked everywhere for her book, and the search took her deeper into the closet's back corners. She couldn't find her paper doll book, but she did find a wooden box, one she had never seen before. Curious, the girl pulled the box from the back corner into the bright light of the room.

Kiki carefully opened its hinged top, and the first thing she noticed was the fragrant, woody smell of cedar. Inside, she found embroidered handkerchiefs, crocheted medallions and little figures dressed as Greek peasants. There was an old photo of a young woman standing in front of a small church. Kiki was pretty sure that she had found the box Mama had brought with her from Greece to America many years ago. The last thing she found was a pair of wire rimmed glasses with rose-colored lenses.

Kiki took the glasses from the bottom of the box and tried them on. She was surprised that they fit her perfectly. How beautiful the world looked through the pink lenses. She replaced all the treasures with great care and carefully put the cedar box back in its place. Mama had once told the children about her box of treasures but no one had seen it before and Kiki kept its secret close to her heart.

That night Kiki had a very vivid dream. Mama was a young woman and she was crying. She appeared all-alone in the world, and walked into the little church to pray for comfort. Her mother wore a coat the priest had given her for the long journey to America. Exhausted and frightened about an unsure future, she lay down on a bench and fell asleep.

Kiki watched as an angel appeared and looked down on Mama with deep compassion. As she looked at Mama, the angel reached into the folds of her garment to reveal rose colored glasses. As the angel placed the glasses in Mama's coat pocket, the dream dissolved away.

When Kiki woke the next morning, she remembered her dream, and as soon as she had a chance, she retrieved the rose colored glasses from the box and placed them in her pocket. Now, she was just like Mama, in possession of a gift from the angels. The girl carried the glasses with her and put them on when no one was watching. First, she looked at the plants and insects in the garden and they all looked magical. She felt she could see deeply into the heart of everything.

Kiki wandered around the garden enchanted. Then Mama surprised her, coming out to pick herbs for her cooking. Kiki hid behind a camellia bush just in time. As she gazed through the rose colored glasses, she saw the hidden side of Mama, sweet tempered, gay, and so artistic. Kiki fell in love with her mother all over again and vowed to be just like this new vision of Mama.

Kiki ran back into the house and up the stairs to Mama's room. She pulled the box out of the closet so she could replace the glasses. Mama, curious as to what all the running was about, followed her into the room.

Stunned, Kiki froze and then stammered, "Mama, look what I found."

"Yes. I see," Mama answered, "the box I carried from Greece to America."

"Mama, look what I found inside," Kiki said as she pulled out the rose colored glasses. "Please may I have them?"

"Yes," answered Mama, "but I warn you. They will give you an unrealistic view of this challenging world.

You must face life's responsibilities and not live in a world of illusions." Kiki put the glasses on and ran to Mama giving her a big hug.

"Thank you, Mama. I will be careful," Kiki exclaimed as she ran for the door. "No running in the house," Mama scolded and Kiki's run turned into graceful, light-hearted skipping. Mama watched with fascination. She had always thought of Kiki as somewhat clumsy, but now she saw only smooth, coordinated movements. That was the beginning of Kiki's transformation. As time went by and she continued to look through the glasses, things began to change. The more she saw the beauty in the world, the more her own beauty shone forth. Mama was amazed to see her beautiful daughter excel as Kiki fulfilled her vow to be sweet, artistic, and refined just like her Mama. The more Mama recognized the reflection of her own true self in her daughter, the more she relaxed and let her own true self show.

There came a time when Kiki no longer needed the rose colored glasses to see the best in the world and everyone around her. It had become her true nature to do so. Everyone Kiki laid eyes on was transformed. They all felt a loving gaze deep in their hearts and rejoiced to be recognized for who they truly were. They in turn, gazed at others with love, and that is how the world eventually transformed and fulfilled the gift of the rose colored glasses. As for the glasses, the angel retrieved them and kept them safe for a day the world may need another reminder of beauty and love.

~ ~ ~ KEY to a New World ~ ~ ~

See The Beauty

THE GIFT

DAUGHTERS, AWAKE!" THE DEMIGOD, Asklepios, exclaimed, as he exploded into the large room where his five daughters lay on their sleeping couches. They were all descendants of the god Apollo who had blessed Asklepios with the knowledge of healing and medicinal herbs. Now, the deity paced the room impatiently. The girls' eyes fluttered open as each sat up to see what all the commotion was about. "What is it Father?" the oldest daughter asked.

"I have just come from my morning prayers and Apollo has charged us with a task. We are to build a healing temple and you will each have a purpose to fulfill," he exclaimed.

The girls looked at each other with furrowed brows. Up until now, their life had been one of luxury and leisure. Their beautiful home was perched on a mountaintop and shrouded with clouds. You could stand on the edge of the portico and look down on the cloud tops as the sun warmed and the breezes cooled their abode. Even the girls were of the substance of clouds and did not fully materialize on Earth.

"Quickly girls, dress and come to the dining hall so we may talk of our plans," Asklepios said. As he hurriedly left the room, his wispy robes swirled with agitation and purpose.

The girls rose, splashed their faces with water mist, and dressed in their own cloudlike garments. Panacea, the oldest, combed her long locks, leaving them to flow freely down her back. Hygeia wrapped her hair in a knot at the nape of her neck. Iaso and Aceso loosely tied their hair back. Aegle was the only one to pile her hair on top of her head and adorn it with strings of translucent pearls. Together, they gracefully made their way to the hall, feet never touching the ground.

Asklepios was standing at a large table with parchment drawings stretched before him. "Look Daughters, we must inspire men to create the first healing temple," he explained. "I will find the greatest builder in the land to raise this new hope for mankind. Meanwhile, you will each train in the gifts you will represent and for which you will be responsible."

Panacea would train in healing herbs and be responsible for the healing remedies. Hygeia would learn methods of cleanliness and personify good health. Aceso would train in the curing systems and healing methods. Iaso would learn the ways of recuperation and renewal. Aegle, the youngest of the sisters, would represent the glow of good health. She was responsible for maintaining the gift of radiance.

That night Asklepios visited the dreams of the most gifted builder in the land and left the parchments nestled in the sleeping man's arms. The beautiful healing temple was built to the exact specifications of the parchments and with the help of Apollo to quicken its pace. The temple was surrounded by mineral springs and serene vistas. When all was complete, Asklepios and his daughters descended from their mountain top and materialized into their earthly forms.

They created healing treatments that would be the template for healing anyone who made the pilgrimage to the temple. The first order from Asklepios was purification of body, mind, and spirit. Hygeia oversaw this task and devised a treatment protocol of baths, meditations, exercise, and simple meals for the first patient. Her treatments would create balance and would be a clean starting point for the next step.

After the purification, the patient was taken to the dreaming chamber where a dream state was induced. Panacea and Aseco sat on either side of the patient as he slept and they whispered cures of medicines, herbs, and procedures. When the patient awoke, he recounted the instructions from his dream and Iaso oversaw his recuperation. The last daughter to bring her gift was Aegle. She held a mirror before the patient so that he could see the reflection of his healthy glow. It was a finishing touch with an impact that would linger and become the symbol of his healing journey.

Asklepios was well pleased, and many healing temples were built to serve all the people in the land. Once physicians and attendants were trained, the family left the material world and returned to their home above the clouds. Throughout the centuries, they watched over a great lineage of healing masters and were always ready to inspire and guide.

The gift of health is available to you as you remember to tap into your own innate healing abilities. Those who watch over you extend an invitation. Purify your daily habits, attending to your body's simple needs. Imagine standing in front of a waterfall as its healing mists envelop and infuse you with cleansing ions. Relax, release, and surrender to the stillness of your center. Listen, as you dream, for the whispers that guide you on your own particular path to balance. Witness the rejuvenation and renewal as your body, mind, and spirit repair and rebuild. Be the radiance that reflects this gift of the gods and live in gratitude.

~ ~ ~ KEY to a New World ~ ~ ~

Be The Radiance Of Health

THE CHOICE

RAVI RAN OUT THE FRONT DOOR OF THE family cottage, tears streaming down her face. Her parents were arguing again, and it had everything to do with her. The year before, her father had given her the glorious gift of a horse. She was the apple of his eye and his favored child. What a wonderful year it had been—filled with love and happiness. Ravi spent all her time with her beloved horse, ignoring her mother's feeble pleas for help with the many household responsibilities. Her father was more lenient. "Let her do what she wants," he would say. He loved to see his daughter so happy and free, exactly as he wished he could be. Her mother held her tongue, doubled down, and did all the household chores herself.

The year went by with one person carefree, one wishing he could be so, and another carrying the extra burden. This precarious balance continued until the fragile structure was rocked when Ravi's Father suffered a mysterious illness. Now, even more of the burden fell on the Mother, and she reached her breaking point.

"The horse must go," she demanded and the Father lost the argument as his strength diminished.

Ravi listened with the realization that her beautiful life was crumbling before her eyes. She ran from the cottage and into the forest to escape this dreadful new reality. The path was familiar so she paid no attention to it as she ran with deep sobs and a pounding heart. When she finally stopped, Ravi was in a part of the forest she didn't recognize. She stumbled through the trees half-heartedly looking for something familiar. Lost, and overcome with grief, she fell to the forest floor. All darkened before her eyes as Ravi's world imploded and she became aware only of her own deeply felt emotions.

When she finally looked up, Ravi saw two different paths. One continued into darkness and the other held the slightest promise of light. The choice lay before her, but now anger surrounded her grief, and she chose the darker path. The path was aligned with her feelings, and as she traveled along it, she began to reflect more of the path's darkness. Eventually, she made her way back to the cottage bringing some of the darkness with her. As the years went by, her dark thoughts created in her an increasingly pessimistic outlook, and her life became the prison her thoughts continued to construct. That is the consequence of choosing the dark path because the mind will create whatever one focuses on.

But let us go back to that moment when Ravi looked up from her grief and saw the choice of paths before her. Imagine that she knows that the mind is the builder and able to guide the shattered emotions. Watch her rise and follow the path with the hint of light. See her anger melt away, allowing the deeply felt grief to heal. Notice how her thoughts reflect the light as she finds her way home. Because of her choice, the fabric of her life reflects a positive outlook, and she rises to face any challenge with courage and faith.

So let us take note and surround ourselves with the knowledge that our thoughts can create anything. They can reflect the darkness or they can reflect the light. The choice is ours.

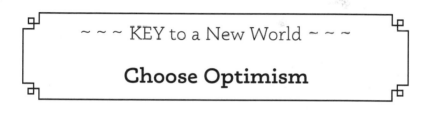

~ ~ ~ KEY to a New World ~ ~ ~

Choose Optimism

A Genesis Story

I N THE CENTER OF A VAST PLAIN SURROUNDED by fields of tall grasses sits a large pond. Many ages ago, Pond was still and reflective. However, with the desire for companionship, it directed some of its waters to transform into large silver fish. Feeling the fish flow and glide through its waters was delightful and for eons this was enough. But now, as Pond glimpsed the reflection of the grasses in its waters, it desired a broader experience. What would it feel like to have a body that could slip in and out of the grasses gracefully, or hooves to stand solidly on the ground? Pond imagined how rich and fascinating this might be. What would it be like to fly high above the plain or run at a full gallop with fire for breath?

With a great churning of its waters, Pond flung four of its largest fish onto its banks. When they landed on the firm ground, they transformed into a great cat, a sturdy ox, a lively horse, and a soaring eagle. Pond was delighted with its creations and settled into stillness to enjoy these new experiences.

The four creatures eyed one another distrustfully as each was so different from the others. Cat slinked in and out of the grasses around the edge of the pond. "Look how magnificent I am," she bragged. "I am like water flowing wherever I want on this land." Cat sat down on the edge of the pond in a most regal pose, purring loudly with satisfaction.

Ox snorted loudly with her disdain, "What do you know of the land? I am the personification of this land." The creature's strong hooves created deep indentations in the soft earth around the pond.

Eagle shrieked his disagreement, "You are not free like I am. I can fly high above you all and feel the air rushing across my wings."

Horse neighed his protest, "Who cares for water, air and earth. I am fire and the vitality of life." Quick as lightning, he galloped furiously, breathing fire as he ran circles around the others.

Pond was reveling in all these new experiences. "Remember where you came from," Pond said with a deep and all-embracing voice. "I made you and you are all part of me. I will enjoy you all and you will be my companions forever." However, the separate creatures

had wills of their own, and they continued to confront each other by emphasizing the superior nature of their own qualities.

When, at last, they tired of their arguments, each of the creatures went their own way, traveled the expanse of the great plain and disappeared into the far forests and mountains. Pond was left alone to ponder if the experiment was worth the sadness of separation.

After a time, tragedy struck the land. A fire raged down from the mountains, into the forests and across the plain, devouring the grasses and everything else in its way. The Horse, Ox, Cat, and Eagle raced back to the safety of the pond, the center of their existence. There they stood on the moist banks and pleaded for Pond to save their world.

"I can do nothing beyond the edge of my waters," Pond said. "It is up to you to work together and find the solution."

The four creatures realized that their differences amounted to very little in the face of this calamity, and that they were truly made of the same substance. Understanding this, they banded together, and each took action based on their own unique gift.

First, Cat wove in and out of the grasses along the pond's banks. Around and around she went, encouraging a great swirling of the waters. Next, Ox stamped on the ground with all her might and caused a great upward surge of the waters. Eagle took flight, spiraling around the rising surge. As a huge funnel of water from Pond rose high above the land, Horse galloped furiously around Pond, breathing fire. This caused the water to turn to steam and mist, which then formed into huge

dark clouds. When the clouds could hold no more moisture, rain blanketed the land and extinguished the fire.

The four exhausted creatures lay on the pond's edge, deeply aware of their deep interconnectedness. Now, they understood the power of unity and how much they were dependent on one another. Peace settled over all and this led to a deep satisfaction with life. Pond no longer wondered about the wisdom of its experiment. It had been a wonderful success and now the way was clear for love to blossom on Earth.

~ ~ ~ KEY to a New World ~ ~ ~

Come Back To Source

THE MAGIC FORMULA

A STRANGER WALKED THROUGH THE TOWN looking for a particular road. He carried a pole across his shoulders with a sack tied on each end. Curious townspeople peeked through windows and some stepped out front doors. The stranger acknowledged them with a nod of his head but he didn't stop to talk. He seemed to know exactly where he was going, and when he found the particular road he sought, he nodded as he looked back at the townspeople one last time.

Later that day some of the townspeople gathered together to speculate on the identity of the stranger. He seemed to know where he was going, and he looked familiar. There was only one property at the end of that road, and it had been abandoned for over 30 years. Most remembered the family who owned the land, and they were not proud of their memories.

The stranger walked to the end of the road and stood on the property's boundary. Memories of sadder times flooded his mind and heart. His ancestors had owned this land for generations. In fact, his immediate family was the last to live on this land, and they had been forced to leave in disgrace. With his parents gone and his siblings more interested in city life, he had come back to reclaim and transform the home of his childhood. As he took a deep breath and released a loud sigh, he was determined to leave the past behind. The first footstep he placed on the property would be a step towards the realization of a dream and the fulfillment of a promise he made to his dying mother.

"Precious boy, my youngest son," she said, "you have been blessed with a kind heart. Use it well. Care for all around you, and in turn, you will always be taken care of. Go back to our land, reclaim it, and let it be an example of the true wealth of enough. Promise to nurture it as I have nurtured you."

"I promise, Mama," he said as she passed peacefully from this life to the next. Now, with all the knowledge and skills he had gathered over the years, he was ready to initiate a miracle.

"I think he must be the youngest son," said one of the townspeople as he nimbly did the math. The group looked at each other with discomfort. They had all treated the family badly. The family had been the poorest in the town and an easy target for ridicule. The townspeople had made themselves out to be better in every way by looking down on a family that so clearly needed help. Some remembered the youngest son, especially, because they had made fun of his tattered clothes and his learning disabilities. The boy had withdrawn into his own private world and his older siblings had found their own ways of dealing with the stigma of poverty. Finally, the family left to start a new life in a more accepting community.

"That property is in shambles," said a different townsperson. "It is beyond repair." "Don't start with your judgements," said another. "I, for one, will no longer take part in that behavior." Most agreed with this, partly because they were not as well off as they once were. Shrugging their shoulders, they dispersed to their homes, with their own troubles and shortcomings.

It is amazing what can be accomplished with a big, loving heart. The stranger, who everyone now remembered as the youngest son, John, rebuilt the house and mended the fence around the property. He cleared the brush and tended to the trees. Soon, there was a vegetable garden full of corn, beans, and squash. Flowers bloomed in front of the front door. John built pens and coops for chickens, ducks, and geese. He kept rabbits for the sheer joy of their soft fur. No animal was ever killed on his property; he didn't have the heart to take another's life. But, he did have an abundance of eggs, his favorite food. He took good care of all, and when he stepped back from the daily work and chores, he admired the magical transformation.

Now there was a new problem in the town. The townspeople were envious of what they perceived to be a vast wealth. "There must have been gold in those sacks he carried into town," said one. "How else could he have so much?"

It was agreed that a delegation of townspeople would go to the property and demand a share of the wealth, a tax they said. So, they marched down the road to John's house and right up to his front door to voice their demands. John listened with a sad smile. Then he opened his sacks for all to see. There was no gold.

Instead, there were only packets of seeds. The townspeople looked confused. "How did all this wealth come from these tiny seeds?" they asked.

"Because I have a magic formula," John answered.

"And will you keep it all for yourself?" they countered.

"No, not at all," John said, and he gave each townsperson seeds, vegetables, and eggs. Somewhat satisfied, they left with their gifts. But soon the food and seeds were gone, and the townspeople still felt that someone had more than they did. So, they went back to John and his magic property to demand more.

"This time," John said, "I will give you a greater gift. You may have the magic formula."

The townspeople gathered around expectantly. "Yes, give us the formula!" they cried.

"First, know that you always have enough. Second,

do your work with happiness and gratitude. And third, let your heart be kind and give to those in need," John said. Then, he gave them more seeds and eggs.

This time, when the townspeople went home, they planted the seeds and hatched the eggs. Soon, they all had their own magical properties. The more they appreciated that what they had was enough, the richer they became.

~ ~ ~ KEY to a New World ~ ~ ~

Know You Always Have Enough and Share Your Gifts

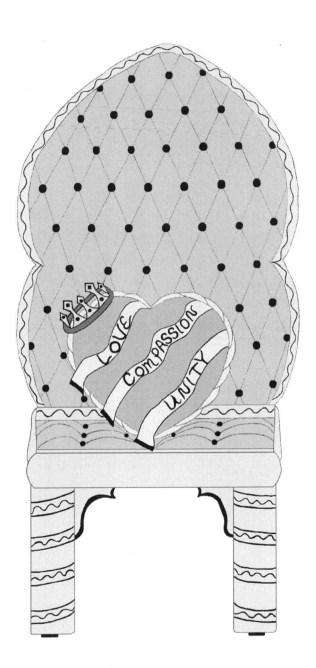

THE GREATEST
TRUTH

ONCE THERE WAS A KING WHO RULED A FAIR land. The people loved him because he was just, compassionate, and wise. The King had spent years building successful towns and cultivating the lush countryside, but now it was time for him to consider which of his sons would succeed him. All three sons were possible candidates, and he was certain the remaining two would support the one who would become King. However, he could not decide which son was best suited to be king, so he devised a quest. He called for his sons, and as they stood before him, he explained the plan.

"I wish to know what the truth is," he said. "Whoever finds the greatest truth will be the next King."

The three sons looked at each other with excitement. They loved a good contest, and they were eager to please their father. The young men shook hands, wished each other good luck, and departed in separate directions to search for the best answer.

The King's only daughter watched and listened from the sidelines. She also wanted to be part of the contest. So, when her brothers departed, she ran to her father.

"Please, Father," she begged, "let me look for the greatest truth, too."

The King ruled over a progressive land but he had not thought of his daughter as a candidate. He considered her request for a moment and then agreed. Whoever returned with the greatest truth would deserve to rule.

The first Son thought he was the best candidate for the throne. He preferred simple answers to complex questions and approached any problem with great organization. Like his father, he was just, and had a strong sense of right and wrong. This son was drawn to travel through the desert because it was straightforward in its uniformity. The days were hot and the nights were cold. It was a land of opposites, and he was sure he would find a truth easy to understand. The first Son was methodical in his search, and he asked the opinion of every person he met. When he considered all the answers, he decided that the best one came from a wise man who understood the simplicity of the desert.

"Look around at how extreme this land is," the wise man said. "There is good and there is evil. Everything is one or the other. You will have a great, ordered land when everything is in its proper category." This is the greatest truth, the first Son thought.

The second Son thought that he would be best to rule the land because he was calm and thoughtful. Like his father, he was wise. He was a good listener, and he could consider all sides of any problem. This son was drawn to travel through a fertile land with many secluded caves. He hoped to discover the greatest truth in one of these quiet retreats and visited many caves listening for the answer. But he wasn't satisfied. The answers he heard only led to more questions. When he entered the last cave, however, he was surprised to see that it was already occupied. The sage in the cave slowly opened his eyes and roused himself from a deep silence. Before the second Son could apologize for the intrusion, the sage spoke.

"You must rid yourself of all desire," he said. "You will have a peaceful land when the people know deep silence and banish unnecessary desire."

The second Son was amazed to hear this answer. He hadn't even voiced the question. This must be the greatest truth, he thought. It was destined that he would enter this last cave and finally hear an answer that led to no more questions.

The third Son journeyed for many days until he arrived at a great bustling city. Like his father, he knew how to build thriving towns. He thought that he was the best candidate because he was good at what mattered most, commerce and growth. He thrived in a competition. He had ambition and a hunger for more. The third Son walked the streets of the great city. I must find the man responsible for these tall buildings, he thought. He asked many citizens for directions, and after more than a few left and right turns, he stood before the tallest building.

"I must talk to the man who has accomplished so much," he demanded and the doorman allowed his entry.

"I must have an audience with the man who constructed this building," he demanded and the elevator attendant took him to the highest floor.

"I must see this man who will have the answers," he demanded and the receptionist opened the office door. The businessman sat behind an enormous desk. The third Son was jubilant.

"I have looked all over this land for the greatest truth and I see what you have accomplished in this grand city," he said. "What is your answer?"

"You've asked the million dollar question," the businessman said. "You must find the greatest man, the one who owns the tallest buildings and has the most money. You will have a great land when all follow with no questions asked. This is the greatest truth."

The third Son was excited by this answer, and he believed every word. He was sure he had found the greatest truth.

The daughter didn't journey at all. She simply walked to the beautiful park surrounding her father's palace. She sat on her favorite bench and watched as the gardener worked. She thought about her question and the many possible answers. None seemed right and she sighed loudly. The gardener looked up from his pruning to see a lovely but troubled young woman. He was a kind and caring man so he approached the bench and asked if he could help.

"Do you know what the greatest truth is?" asked the daughter.

"Well," answered the gardener, "You are asking the wrong question. A better question is how do you know what the truth is?"

The Daughter was intrigued. "Tell me more," she said.

"I think the greatest truth is the one that can be true for everyone," he continued. "We each have a different path to that truth. You will recognize it when you feel unity with all around you. You will know it when you feel empathy, compassion, and love."

The Daughter closed her eyes and allowed herself to drop down to the center of her awareness. She knew who she was in this place, and as she opened her eyes, she saw the beautiful park and each of the little details that made it what it was. She looked at the gardener and saw a gentle man content to be great in his own self-knowledge. This is the greatest truth, she thought. Know yourself, love yourself, and allow the same for all around you.

The three Sons and the Daughter stood before the King eager to present the answers they had found. Each Son was certain he had the best answer. The Daughter only knew that her answer gave her a clarity she had never experienced before. She was now deeply aware of herself and all around her.

The first Son stepped forward and said, "The greatest truth I found is that all can be categorized as good or evil. This will shape a great and ordered society." The King considered his first son's answer. "The problem with that," he said, "is that it would create divisions among the people. This land will never be great as long as judgement divides the people."

The first Son was disappointed that his answer was so swiftly discarded but he stepped back to allow the second Son his turn.

"The greatest truth I found," said the second Son, "is to live with no desires. This will bring great peace to the people."

The King contemplated this truth, but after a few moments he realized its serious flaw. "If desires were banished there would be no motivation," he said. "Nothing would be created." The second Son realized his father was right and stepped back to allow the third Son his turn.

"The greatest truth is to find the greatest man to lead the people to material wealth," the third Son explained. "This man would succeed in bringing material success to everyone as long as all followed with no questions asked."

The King was silent before he replied, "I do not want to see the people blindly follow such a one-dimensional man. What you say assumes that material wealth is all that is needed." The third Son was disappointed, but he had to admit his father was right: money alone would not make the people happy.

The Daughter stepped forward to share her answer. "The greatest truth that I found is to follow your own path to the inner place that can be true for everyone, a place of unity and love."

The King nodded his agreement, "This is the way our people could have all the peace, wealth, and order they would ever want. They will be free to know themselves and allow the same for all others. Daughter, you have found the greatest truth and I proclaim you the next ruler of this Land."

The King was confident that he had chosen the one who could best lead with love and compassion. His Daughter would always surround herself with people who were best suited for the positions they held.

The Sons' talents were not wasted. The first became the Kingdom's chief administrator since he understood the importance of organization. The second became the Kingdom's chief spiritual advisor because he knew the importance of peace. The third was put in charge of the Kingdom's treasury and all the great building projects. All would work together for the greatest success. This was the formula for a great land. The quest had uncovered the greatest truth: know yourself.

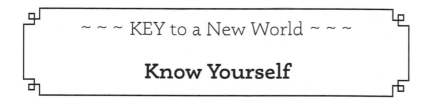

~ ~ ~ KEY to a New World ~ ~ ~

Know Yourself

DOWN THE
MOUNTAIN

O N THIS NEW EVENING, OUR FAMILY SAT around the campfire eagerly awaiting the next story. We peered into the flames, waiting for a figure to materialize in the dim light beyond and were almost disappointed when the original Storyteller appeared.

"The stories are finished for now," she said. "They are yours to do with as you please. But there is one final story. You and your journey are the last story, and I leave you with one more key." The Storyteller, her eyes shining, looked directly at each of us as she said, "Follow the way. Be the love. This is the gift of the last key." Then she faded back into the darkness beyond the campfire.

My family was quiet for a while as we gazed into the fire, each of us integrating the stories in our own way. My brother and I were disappointed that the magical evenings around the fire had come to an end. We had quite a collection of keys to help us recall the stories, but as Mom gazed at us, I knew she was wondering what new experiences she could present. Then an idea occurred to her.

"Let's retell the stories," she said. She stood, walked

to the cabin, and returned with a writing pad and pen. Each night, my family retold a story, with each of us remembering and adding details. Mom wrote down every word, and in this way, the stories were reconstructed in the retelling. My brother and I were inspired to draw pictures, and when the pages were ready, Dad bound them all together into a book.

Soon it was time to leave the mountain and return to the city, and we spent our last night around the campfire passing the book to each other, admiring what we had created. The book was a symbol of our magical time in the mountains. The keys would remind us what was important. Now, we were ready to help rebuild the world.

The next morning, our family packed for the journey back home. We slowly carried our belongings from the cabin to the truck, reluctant to leave the safety of the mountains. When it was finally time to go, Mom and Dad opened the pick-up truck doors and waited for my brother and me to climb into the back seat. But I had a different idea.

"Dad, let me lead. I know the way," I said as I walked to the front of the truck. My brother joined me and together we took the first steps down the mountain and into our future.

"Great idea," Dad answered. "We will follow and when you get tired, we will pick you up."

~ ~ ~ KEY to a New World ~ ~ ~

Follow The Way, Be The Love

KEYS TO A NEW WORLD

Ask and You Will Receive

Let Yourself Dream

Believe In Yourself

Transform Your Fear

Follow The Light

Open Your Heart

Allow The Miracle Of Life

Expand Your Horizons

Listen For Your Purpose

Embrace Empathy and Equality

See The Beauty

Be The Radiance Of Health

Choose Optimism

Come Back To Source

Know You Always Have Enough and Share Your Gifts

Know Yourself

Follow The Way, Be The Love

About the Author and Illustrator

GENIE VALEN lives in Santa Fe, New Mexico with her husband, Patrick. Her life experiences include a career as a professional classical dancer and teacher, hypnotherapy training, and a practice in the healing art of skincare. She founded Creative Dance Adventures, inspiring young children in Los Angeles and Santa Fe. Genie hopes to continue to inspire children of all ages with her stories.

LESLIE COOK began her professional career as a dancer with North Carolina Dance Theater. She continued in the film and television industry for over 30 years as a dancer, choreographer, and actress. Currently, she lives in Santa Fe, New Mexico where she enjoys the many facets of culture and creativity.